RECAPTURE OWERRI!

O. ANAH & E. EMEABA

copyright © 2019 by O. Anah & E. Emeaba

Recapture Owerri is a work of military adventure pulp fiction. While it takes place against the backdrop of the Biafra War, the incident recorded Were a real event. Detail have been Changed and fictitious character and element have been added for dramatic purposes. Names, character, and some incidents are either the product of the author's imagination, or are used fictitiously. Any resemblance to actual persons, living or dead is entirely coincidental. In other Words, there are probably numerous things that are not one hundred percent accurate and real World in these pages. That's okay. It's not intended to be an in-depth, hundred percent accurate book.
Hopefully you'll excuse any literary License.

Printed in the federal republic of Nigeria

TABLE OF CONTENTS

PART ONE

Barely six years after Nigeria wrested independence from British colonial government, some young but, in retrospect, crazy majors in the Nigeria army – mostly of Ibo extraction – up and started killing the politicians of the day claiming the civilians were steering the Nigerian state wrong. It turned out that those so killed were mostly name-brand Hausa-Fulani politicians.

The rebellious soldiers later claimed all the Nigerian politicians, irrespective of tribe, were slated to be killed; but then, the coup makers for some weird reason, did not kill any Ibo politician, which justifiably angered the Hausa Fulani tribal elements who never really liked the Ibo brashness and aggressive individualism. And so, the tribal massacres began. The Hausa-Fulani Muslims in the north, naturally adept with knives from practice in the art of butchering cattle, hacked to death every Ibo person they could lay their hands on. Within days, an approximate 30,000 Ibo men, women, and children were variously maimed, decapitated or slaughtered. Some said their eyes were gouged out; and they were made to eat their own eyes.

Then, northern elements in the Federal Army singled out their defenceless colleagues of Ibo extraction and shot them in the barracks. While the military governor of northern Nigeria, Lieutenant Colonel Hassan Katsina conveniently allowed the killing to go on, the military governor of eastern Nigeria, Lieutenant Colonel Odumegwu Ojukwu figured if the Ibo were going to be killed as it appeared, all Ibos who had been chased into eastern Nigeria couldn't possibly be a part of a country that would kill them on sight. He consulted with the people and it was agreed he should declare eastern Nigeria an independent country of Biafra. The Federal Government, made up of recently promoted soldiers who suddenly found themselves wearing shoes far bigger their feet, would not hear of it. Meanwhile, pockets of Ibo civilians were being hunted down and killed wherever they may be. When this was not enough reprisal for them, the northern military hawks had deceived themselves into believing that they could also chase them into the Ibo country to finish what they had started. What they did not know was that the people they'd be fighting in Biafra would be nothing like the defenceless ones they shot up in the northern army barracks which had resulted in an outcome that resembled a victory to them.

The Federal army attacked the newly independent Biafra country thinking it was made of civilians. Former Ibo Federal officers who had been chased back to the eastern region, mobilised and trained ready volunteers who were prepared to defend themselves from what seemed as an attempt to annihilate a whole tribe of people. And the Biafra war was on...

The Biafran Army withstood everything that the Federal army dished out to them; and even made some pre-emptive incursions into the Midwest en route to Lagos – the seat of the Federal military government – a move that scared the devil out of the leadership. When the Federal army confronted the determined Ibo people, they quickly discovered that frontal warfare couldn't possibly be the best way to fight the ingenious Biafrans who had started manufacturing their own weapons of war. And so, the Federal troops cordoned off the southern reaches to Biafra, blockading supply route that was necessary to fight the war and with it, all food shipments going into Biafra. They simply sat back and gloatingly watched Ibo people – particularly the children – starve by the numbers.

The Federal government also got international support from the Russians who were hoping to get in on the ground level in order to enhance their chances of partaking in the global scramble for Africa which they missed out when the German Bismarck divvied up the continent like some extra-large pepperoni pizza. Biafra improvised as the Russians supplied Ilyushin 28s and the British supplied MiG-17s. and crewed the aircrafts with Egyptian mercenaries who had a reputation for bombing civilians in open air markets. Even by third world criteria, the Federal Air Force was not fighting fair as it conveniently avoided military targets only to strafe hospitals and sick bays, bomb refugee camps, and drop napalm bombs on fleeing civilians and on open air church services.

X   X   X

By the July of 1968, Biafra was virtually surrounded and the sea route into the new country cordoned off preventing marine traffic activities going in or out. It was just a question of waiting it out for the Biafrans to starve out. The Federal 3rd Division and its commander, Colonel Benjamin Adekunle that easily captured Bonny, Port-Harcourt and Calabar, garnering a reputation for himself as the one to force seceding Biafrans back had been fooled by the ease with which he took those coastal areas. The minority natives of the captured areas had for years believed the Ibos were their problem and had cooperated with the invading Federal forces with that erroneous belief that as soon as the enterprising Ibos were flushed out of their neighbourhood, the spoils would be handed to them. The natives had shown the 3rd Division how to get into and manoeuvre the creeks, thus subverting Biafra's defence systems there. Worse Colonel Adekunle had underrated the Biafrans, forgetting those were desperate people defending their home turf from invaders. He was heard to have described the Ibo as spineless people with not enough fire power in their belly. This was the worst opinion to have about the Ibo whose war time leaders were previously his commanding officers before the war that shot him to limelight. He had suddenly forgotten.

The local press did him in – painting him with the wrong colours and he believed them. The charismatic war commander with the can-do attitude suddenly changed when with that singular victory, and lulled by the encomiums of the press and the Federal high command, Adekule had thought himself an invincible local Caesar. He bragged and ranted about his invincibility and how he was going to starve the Ibo to death. He was said to have said, "I want to see no Red Cross, no Caritas, no World Council of Churches, no Pope, no missionary and no UN delegation. I want to prevent even one Ibo from having even one piece to eat before their capitulation. We shoot at everything that moves and when our troops march into the centre of Ibo territory, we shoot at everything even at things that do not move." He was able to do that, and it worked for him.

And so, even without authorization from his commanding officers at the supreme headquarters, he began making plans for an invasion of the cities of Aba, Owerri and Umuahia in a massive military attack operation he had nicknamed "Operation OAU"

In his loudmouth manner, he had stated that he would be able to capture all three cities in two weeks, Adekunle's strategy was to surround a city and starve it into submission before attacking its weakened defenders. After 12 days of violent fighting in Aba, his unilaterally christened 3rd marine Commandoes managed to capture the city followed by Owerri two days later. When he was pushed back at Umuahia, his units retreated to Owerri and set up defences in and around the city in their usual starve out, emasculate, and pound-to-submission procedure.

In his blind belief of his invincibility, he started making decisions that saw to the decimation of the troops of his self-styled marine commandos leading to mass deaths among his men; enough for some to desert and his officers to request for transfers to other units. And so, as he yearned to enter the Ibo heartland, he refused every cautionary taps on his shoulders to apply the brakes. He was hell-bent on entering the Ibo country. Analogous to Lieutenant Colonel Murtala Muhammad when he was raring to enter the Ibo country through Asaba, he did not listen to sound advice for he had made up his mind to go in and kill as many Ibo as possible. Both results had been tragic – the Biafran decimation of men under their divisions.

X   X   X

When the Federal forces entered the middle of Ibo country they had planned on winning using their usual traditional methods; thinking that the war would be won by conquering land. Of course, the Federal troops had never been in any war before and therefore were not used to the jungle terrain. The Biafrans realized that the only way the war could be won was through a method of wearing away. In other words, a war was not won by who had more land, but whomever eliminated more opposing troops. Biafran troops were actually very successful in using this method; they killed over two times as many soldiers as they lost. However this style of warfare enraged many Federal troops that they started targeting civilians and shooting up market places as well in order to even up the score.

The Biafrans had conducted numerous attacks and defensive manoeuvres, generally having the advantage of choosing the time and place for such operations. At a point, about 75 percent of all engagements against Federal forces were initiated by the Biafrans who generally had two approaches to the war: The first, inflict maximum losses on the Federal forces by expending resources in attacks (ambushes, raids, and plain harassments), or in defensive operations (digging in to fight, draining the opponents and then retreating in the face of superior or overwhelming fire power). In such situations, attacks could be scaled up or down depending on a lot of factors, including the importance of the area so defended. The second approach was to completely avoid a battle unless there was a chance of success. It was foolhardy to expend scarce ammunition.

PART TWO

And so, when without adequate preparation Adekunle plunged his men into his Operation OAU in an attempt at a mop-it-up operation, he did capture Owerri because the Biafrans let him for a reason.

Still flying from the adrenaline euphoria of capturing Port-Harcourt and Calabar, Adekunle and his Federal 3rd Division pushed west, conquering everything in their way through the Niger Delta and beyond. With Port-Harcourt this close to the sea, the 3rd Division got help from the naval ships anchored there. A combined Army and Navy bombardment rained death on Biafran positions making it impossible for them to put up any form of resistance. The Biafran forces retreated to Aba, leaving Owerri wide open for the 16th Brigade of the Federal 3rd Division led by Colonel E. A. Etuk to capture Owerri. This turned out to be a short-lived victory.

By spreading his division thin trying to capture the whole of Biafran by himself, Adekunle could not hold all the cities he had captured earlier had been willing to help mop up straggling Biafrans and making their rear safe, but not so in the core Ibo areas. He had made an attempt to take on Umuahia but discovered to his chagrin that the terrain around Umuahia consisted of expenses of vast jungles and rivers that were scattered with mines and determined Biafrans soldiers who had just made the last stand.

Colonel Adekunle could not believe the doggedness of the opponents he encountered when he got into Ibo country, and the two sides traded gunfire and artillery, causing mass losses on both sides. Adekunle suffered so much losses that he was short of men to continue his foolhardy offensive into Biafra. He had gone on radio to inform the army headquarters he needed re-enforcements or his entire division would be at risk of total destruction. Meanwhile, Adekunle's brashness was beginning to grate in the ears of his superior officers who were reluctant to give him more for him to use as canon fodders for the Biafrans. They won't give him any reinforcements. With that many losses and no new men coming in to his aid, Adekunle took his division and retreated to Port-Harcourt. That single act had had the consequence of isolating the 16th Brigade of his command inside Owerri and exposed to certain death.

Biafran Brigadier Alexander Madiebo surrounded Owerri, and in so doing, trapped the 3,000-man Federal troops of the 16th Brigade inside the city. He had borrowed a leaf from Adekunle's strategy and encircled Owerri, effectively making it impossible for Federal supply convoys to enter the city for resupply. The convoy that made an attempt at resupply, encountered two formidable forces: the rains which had come with a vengeance, pounding the red dirt Ibo roads and making them virtually unusable by motorized vehicles, and the die-hard members of the Biafran Organization of Freedom Fighters abbreviated to BOFF who were running the neighbourhood looking for something to destroy, blow up, or just plain kill in a brutal way.

X   X   X

They were five dangerous men you do not want to piss off, but they were pissed off already as each had an axe to grind with the invading Federal forces who had wronged them in one way or the other. Their BOFF vehicle was a Land Rover R- 01 light utility vehicle a cross between a light truck and a tractor. Built on the American Jeep chassis, but wider, heavier and faster than its American inspiration, the vehicle had become standard light military vehicle with the capability of seating seven people. This particular vehicle was the Long-Range Desert Patrol type that was originally used by the British SAS for desert patrol special operations and had been donated to the Federal army. It had been converted for combat use by being stripped of doors and windscreens and fitted with grenade launchers, a machine gun mounting ring and a long-range fuel tank and water tanks. The Land Rover used the 2.25-litre four- cylinder petrol engine on a leaf-spring suspension with selectable two or four-wheel drive

(4WD). It was started with a front hand crank where a man would go to the front of the vehicle, stick a curved cranking rod in the front below the grill and give it a round turn that would kick-start the engine.

It had been raining all day, and the men were in a great big zero-visibility rain squall bank as the Land-Rover was rolling down an unpaved road somewhere, a long way behind the enemy lines. The truck was armed to the teeth looking for something to shoot. Driving down a federal main supply route between Port-Harcourt and Owerri in the middle of a rainstorm night behind enemy lines was not for the faint of heart. But then, the Federals were afraid of fighting in the night inside Ibo country, too.

The group of five BOFF operatives patrolling the country side in a Land-Rover, drove up on a group of trucks pulled off the waterlogged red mud road to the left. It was a Federal resupply convoy that had been attempting to run at night, but the rains had made travel on the muddied roads almost impossible. Suddenly, the BOFF had arrived on the scene unannounced, out of the dark, in the middle of the night with bad attitude and intentions.

Major Kalu Obasi leading the group of dangerous men could not tell how many trucks were in the convoy. Visibility was limited to the vehicles parked closest to the road a few feet away. The instant Major Obasi recognized the silhouette of the fender through the squall, two things happened simultaneously: he realized it had the dark-green painted fender of the British hand-me-down Bedford M- type 4 ton trucks with high tyres, and he opened up with his Vickers Class K machine gun. The 4-speed truck had been an ideal light truck with chassis, cab and a flatbed that could convert to a troop carrier, a tipper, or a recovery vehicle, and it was known to be used by the Federal forces. Obasi noted that anybody driving these trucks was out to kill Biafrans. His Vickers Class K was a rapid-firing machine gun that used a locking tilting breechblock with an adjustable rate of fire between 950 and 1,200 rounds per minute. The gun, fitted with a single spade grip at the rear of the receiver, and a trigger to control fire below the receiver, was mounted on twin pindles on the Land-Rover jeep and was capable of deadly results wherever it hit.

Without asking why the commanding officer was shooting, or even what he was shooting at, Major Chinedum Iheanetu commenced firing crisp bursts with his Bren gun, and the one-handed mechanic, Captain Ekelediri Onyema ex-Nigerian army Corporal, an experienced operator with more military training than anyone in BOFF, was blazing away, taking out his one-handed frustrations with his mounted machine gun, having lost the hand when marauding northern elements had chopped his left arm off trying to have him killed for being Ibo in the north.

Citing his experience in the Federal army where he had been a Corporal, the Biafran recruiting officers had taken a look at his one arm and written him off as useless for the army. Then, a discerning recruiter figured he could do well as a trainer. He was able to churn out many Biafran soldiers and kept telling them to go get his arm back from those he started describing as 'people who do not know God.' To give him enough power to handle his recruits, he was promoted Captain.

Each recruit set got a different version which increased in gore and details as the war wore on. He had several versions of how he lost his arm. In one version he had said, "I was stationed at an army barrack in the north and a colleague had come after me with what I thought was a stick. I had parried the blow when it came at me hoping to fend off a club strike to my head. It was only when my left hand fell off two inches below my elbow and landed on the dusty arid northern earth did I know the fellow was not only out to just beat me, but to behead me. I want you all to go out there and find his brothers and behead them for me."

On the other side of the Land-Rover, Akwaba, the ace Biafran army antiaircraft gunner who had volunteered for duty with BOFF, was working his pedestal-mounted 20mm Oerlikons anti-tank weapon. Designed to be manually aimed by a gunner with a 30-round drum magazine, and with a rate of fire of 500 rpm and an effective firing range of 1,600 yards, Akwaba worked the trigger as the cannons roared—KWAPU, KWAPU, KWAPU—t0 lethal effect. His name was actually Captain Ukariwo, but he liked the sound of that Ghanaian word for Welcome and made a nickname out of it. Each gunner in the patrol Land-Rover engaged as they came to bear. In a slow motion drive-by shooting tactics the Vickers, the Bren, and the Oerlikons were putting out a blizzard of tracers at point-blank range.

The roar of so many massed machine guns was tremendous. Several Federal army trucks started to burn as the KWAPU, KWAPU, KWAPU; UNUDUM filled the night. Then, there was a KPOOOOOM as a gas tank exploded. It sounded like a thousand-pound bomb as the flame blossomed in an orange and red kaleidoscope of colours. The canvas tops of some trucks caught fire in a surprizing petrol-fuelled blaze that spread from truck to truck. Those trucks loaded with ammunition started to cook off something fearful, combining with the belts of ammo on the BOFF machine guns to create a confusing bowel-loosening horror as tracer, armour piercing and incendiary shrapnel flew every which way. The thin-skinned vehicles were being shredded like can-openers on sardine tins, in a devastating fashion. The men aimed low, taking out both the trucks and the gunners who themselves could not see due to the rain-induced limited visibility.

PART THREE

As the raiding Land-Rover drove by, the last man whose rear-facing Boys anti-tank rifle had not seen action, swung the formidable weapon on those other vehicles in the convoy stacked in the front preparatory to dissuade any one foolhardy enough to want to give chase. The Boys rifle, adequate against light tanks, and light-skinned combat vehicles was useful in knocking holes through walls during street fighting. Poised in the front of the Federal supply convoy was an Alvis Saladin armoured car. Weighing in at 11 ton and capable of 70 km/h on its six-wheeled base, it was not a vehicle anyone would want chasing one after stirring his Hornet's nest.

Corporal Nwawo manning the Boys rifle saw its hulking 76mm spin-stabilized gun barrel and a coaxial mount Browning M2 Machine Gun top mounted behind a 32mm gun shield plate. Most importantly, Corporal Nwawo thought he saw someone trying to get into it. He swung the Boys at the Saladin and started firing. A bolt action rifle fed from a five-shot magazine, the weapon was large and heavy with a bipod at the front and a separate grip below.

Nwawo knew it was effective, but his first two rounds pinged off the armoured vehicle and ricocheted uselessly into the bush. Then, he simply shredded a hand that was trying to scramble into the turret, before concentrating the remaining fire on the right front tire at an angle that was sure to rip off a piece of rubber to render the tyre useless.

The BOFF boys had achieved instantaneous, overwhelming fire superiority and the surprise was total. Being so far away from the fighting in the front lines, none of the Federal truckers ever dreamed they could come under such heavy ground attack. They were in too much of a shock to give chase, or even shoot back, for most of the drivers were unarmed, having left their weapons in their trucks. None made any attempt to retrieve them not having the zeal to fight back as the driver of the raiding force peeled out to get far away from the scene of mayhem. The Land-Rover was nearing sixty miles per hour. The engine whined loudly, protesting the demands of the driver who seemed to have only three speeds—Go-Fast, Go-Faster, and Go-Fastest. He couldn't relax in the calmest of circumstances.

The dirt road was mostly flat but extremely bumpy. The BOFF men were not bothered by the wet and slippery road, for the auxiliary gear in the Land-Rover rose to the occasion. Their heads bobbed forward and back with every bump, like they were in a traditional group dance fest.

X   X   X

Biafran soldiers made their way down the Aba-Umuahia road and managed to capture the entire road along with Aba and thus completely cut off the Federal 16th Brigade unit in Owerri from their parent Division in Port- Harcourt. The road was heavily mined and made practically impossible for any form of motorized vehicle to pass through, thus effectively isolating the 6th Brigade in Owerri.

All of the Biafrans' attempts to dislodge the 16th Brigade from Owerri, simply wasted men and ammunition. The Brigade's Commander, Colonel Etuk who was sustaining an unprecedented heavy loss, maintained his position hoping for reinforcement that would never come. Apparently, his boss Colonel Adekunle was having problems getting the badly needed reinforcement for beefing up his depleted Division.

On one occasion the Biafrans came close to dislodging the Federal troops after a two-day offensive that whittled down the besieged Brigade and forced a tactical retreat. The little real estate captured by the Biafran fighters happened to have clothing and food supplies. The choice was easy to make between continuing to pursue the fleeing Federal troops or simply hunkering down for a decent meal and a change of clothing. While the Biafrans feasted, Colonel Etuk regrouped his men and came back with bad plans. Even at that, the Biafrans still had over 70 percent of the city.

X   X   X

Staff Sergeant Roland Utuk could easily have taken out the commanding officer, but hearing that his name was Etuk, he had had that linguistic-loyalty thing bothering him. He could fool around and kill his own kin even though he was fighting for the wrong side. Instead, he swung the gun looking for an officer-looking fellow. To the naked eye, you could see blurred silhouettes moving around in the distance. A thousand; maybe eight hundred yards away Utuk adjusted the magnification on his sniper day-scope. The Federal officer came into full view. The man was definitely an officer. On each of his shoulder epaulettes was a single dot. At the distance, it was not possible to differentiate between an Eagle for the rank of Major, and a Star for the rank of Second Lieutenant. He was a Federal officer all the same. Utuk snuggled in tight to the stock of his long sniper rifle.

The weapon in Utuk's hands was a British military sniper rifle designated the L115A3 Long Range Rifle.

This was a bolt-action weapon, chambered in with a .338 Magnum (8.59mm) bullet, with an effective range out to 1.2 km. At the top of the rifle was a Schmidt & Bender 25X magnification day-scope. The shot he was going to take was a piece of cake, having done it several times before. Staff Sergeant Utuk was familiar with the rifle.

During his basic 5-week sniper course, he had covered the weapon's rules, judging distance, camouflage and concealment, stalking, map reading and observation, shooting, sniper knowledge and regimental sniper doctrine and tactics. The course had culminated in a two week long practical exercise which included the 'stalk' in which students attempt to infiltrate across 1.5km of terrain, get in position, fire their weapon and withdraw to a safe area, all without being spotted by the instructors. Utuk's practice had turned into a target of opportunity.

He remembered vividly how it had happened. As he prepared to fire at a distant object, a helicopter with Russian markings had suddenly noisily materialized.

One look at his observing instructor, the two men had come to the same conclusions. Russian markings—the Russians who were supplying the Federal troops with the weapons that were being used to kill the Biafrans. Maybe the Russians should get a taste of their own medicine. Utuk had rolled over onto his back and aimed his rifle at the slow-moving chopper.

The pilot had been deceived into believing that the Biafrans had been chased away, and there was none to won-y about in the neighbourhood. As he flew low without care, Utuk composed himself hoping there should be a lot of high-ranking Federal officers in it. He did not know what part of the chopper was the vital part to shoot at so as to crash it. He decided, if no one was flying the machine, it would crash all the same.

He had shot the pilot. Intercepted radio message had it that the dead had included a high-ranking Federal officer, probably the Army Chief of Staff, Colonel Akahhan and his entourage who had come to inspect

Federal liberated areas. The message was simply muted and it was not clear who died but soon after, a new Chief of staff was appointed.

X   X   X

In the chopper, the occupants looked out the window at the devastated landscape result of the Federal troop's scotched-earth war tactics. When the sniper's bullet hit, the chopper pulled up abruptly and dropped sharply, making the passengers' bowels jump as their buttocks involuntarily clenched. It made a sharp vertical climb and banked hard to the left. The principal passenger, Colonel Akahhan fell over sideways. He clung to the floor's metal slats. An alarm in the cockpit began to sound, PEEM, PEEM, PEEM, as the pilot said, "Colonel, we've got Mayday. Our rotor has been hit. It's wobbling. It's not going to hold. We either land or we crash, but we're going down."

"How long do we have?" the Colonel asked, wondering what the Biafrans would do to a captured

Federal Army Chief of Staff if the chopper crashed in Biafra held area.

"Ninety seconds. Maybe. The longer we hold out, the harder we hit," the pilot said, feeling the cyclic control shuddering in his gloved hands.

The Colonel said, "Please don't kill us."

"I'll do my best," the pilot said. They were five hundred feet in the air and a quarter mile to effective rescue. Instantly, the chopper banked hard left and down, and then dropped a hundred feet in a few seconds. They were going down fast. Three hundred feet. Two hundred. "Mayday mayday," the pilot said, "Assume crash positions." In front of him, the ground was coming up fast. The world zoomed by with dizzying speed. They were twenty feet from the ground. The pilot calmly said, "Impact in three, two..."

BOOM! A light flashed. It was white, and enormous, and blinding. It swallowed the chopper whole. The colonel was blasted off his seat by its sheer force. He flew through the interior of the chopper, hit the padded wall behind him and fell to the floor. Everything had gone dim. He could not see. The ground beneath him was pulsating as the chopper's propellers kept trying to rotate even as it dug into the soft forest ground. Suddenly, another light flashed; bigger this time, more forceful. Everything was muted. The Colonel knew instantly that his legs were crushed, and that he was in all probability, paralyzed from the waist down. He suspected that although he couldn't feel it, he was probably bleeding profusely. In the dimness that enveloped him, people he could not see were shrieking as he smelled a mixture of roasted meat and burning rubber as an intense fire engulfed the downed chopper. He vaguely observed that there was no difference between the smell of burning beef and burning human flesh. Morbidly, it occurred to him the two probably tasted the same.

PART FOUR

Inside the beleaguered 16th Brigade in Owerri, Colonel Etuk and his men were are their wit's end. All their attempts to raise the parent Divisional command ended in disaster. He had been ordered to hold the city until relieved. For several months, there had been no attempt to send relief even as he lost men daily. Short of supplies and men, Etuk had a mind to surrender, but information he received about the Biafrans—they never take prisoners. Prisoners meant prison camp, food for the prisoners, and the possibility of the prisoners escaping. There had been stories of how Biafrans simply lined up captured Federal soldiers and hacked off their heads since bullets were for fighting wars. Colonel Etuk knew this and was desperate.

When he contacted his commanding officer, Colonel Adekunle, he had mentioned that using the road from Port- Harcourt to Owerri was impossible, but to use airdrops. The radio communication asking Etuk to set up a drop zone for supplies to be dropped had also been picked up by the Biafran intelligence agency and they had promptly set up a different drop zone. The Federal pilots who were too scared to fly into the Ibo country were not very keen to look around for the right drop zone. This one had just seen a large fire burning as was instructed for a signal, and decided to drop the whole items which were all intercepted by the Biafrans. When the supplies did not arrive, Etuk had gone back to the radio to contact Adekunle to complain the items did not arrive. Adekunle had mistaken the complaints as an attempt to get more, and had characteristically blown a fuse, "You bastard son of a bitch," he had yelled at Etuk, "Do you think you are the only commander I have?"

For several months, Biafrans took possession of over 50 percent of all the air-dropped supplies meant for the 16th Brigade during the siege of Owerri. Meanwhile, every attempt to link up to Owerri from Port-Harcourt was thwarted by the Biafrans.

X   X   X

Today, as Staff Sergeant Utuk peered through his scope and got ready to shoot his daily ration of one-Federal- officer-a-day routine, he slowed his breathing as his heart- rate evened out like a slow-ticking clock. His left eye was shut and his right was looking down the scope. The fingers of his right hand curled around the wood-grain pistol-grip of the weapon as his forefinger rested gently on the trigger. Seven hundred yards away his target was still, unmoving but gesticulating with his hands in an authoritative manner. The morning air was cool and clean. Utuk licked his middle finger and raised it up to feel the movement of the air. With no cross wind to worry about, he aimed at the crosshairs of the scope on the man's right eye.

He had done the mathematics several times before; the average length of a human head and torso was thirty six inches, where the head alone took up to ten of the total. In his sniper training manual, Utuk had read that snipers talk about the fatal T, the region on a target's head where any impact from a bullet would be an instant kill.

From the chin to the nose and either side on each, any round that went through that area would instantly sever the brain stem and spinal cord. A targeted man would be dead before he hit the ground, and nine times out of ten would not even hear the shot that killed him. With a moving target, a torso shot was more reliable, especially since the target area was larger, and any hit to a vital organ was effectively a kill-shot regardless. But the man on the wrong end of the scope that morning was stationary but moving his hands. And he was about to get shot. Utuk liked the spectacular result of a head shot, but this morning, he was not in his joking mode; even though there was no hurry for the troops occupying Owerri to leave, considering their presence had been responsible for good food and good supplies from their air drops, Utuk needed to fulfil his daily quota of one Federal Officer a day routine. On that he squeezed the trigger.

Utuk looked in the day-scope and observed that the officer had just collapsed and a bunch of soldiers were milling around and seeming not to know what was going on. "Bull's eye," Utuk said to his spotter.

The spotter asked the sniper, "How many people have you killed since you started this?" He answered, "I stopped counting my confirmed kills at a hundred.. ."

X   X   X

The commanding officer of the 16th Brigade, Colonel E. A. Etuk had just issued an order that the troop needed to execute a tactical withdrawal. The order had been for all to prepare for the actual en-masse pull out from the besieged city of Owerri. Second in command to Colonel Etuk, Major T. Hamman of the besieged Brigade, had just come out of the briefing room where they had been deliberating on the best way to save themselves. Apparently, they had been written off for dead when the 3rd Division's headquarters did not make any attempt to send help their way.

The Federal 3rd Division had been adept at surrounding a city and starving them for a couple of months before bombarding the place with enough fire power to dissuade any effort at resistance. It had worked for them in the past enough to give their Division commander, Colonel Adekunle a mythical aura of the man that was single-handedly trying to make the country one again. Even schools out west were noted for singing, "One Nigeria; Adekunle Sector" alluding to his prowess in capturing city after city in Biafra's southern seaboard. This time, one of Adekunle's 16th Brigade was taking a dose of the same medicine that they had been noted to dispense. With Biafran forces hunkered down around the city of Owerri, elements of BOFF knew there was no way for reinforcement to go in to save them.

A lot of the 16th Division troops found Jesus, praying for deliverance only for the Biafrans to come at night to harass them with mortar fire. They were not only starved, but also prevented from sleeping a wink. Even the 3rd Division's headquarters had no other plans to relieve their colleagues except to resupply them by air. The commanders knew that no fighting unit could sustain morale, and effectively remain cohesive after having been starved almost to death of not only food but also of spare parts and medical supplies. They knew this because they were the ones that originated that strategy and had successfully used it against the Biafrans.

Surrendering to the Biafrans was not an option. Worse, the Brigade's number was being reduced everyday by insurgency and sniper fire. Out of a Brigade of 3,000 men, you could barely count up to 300 remaining. Pulling out was the best option. Disobeying the Divisional Commander's direct order of "hold until relieved" simply earned one a court-martial. Staying to be captured by the Biafrans earned one a death sentence—an excruciatingly painful death. He had agreed with the pull-out order especially since the Biafran forces were crawling close to their positions, and killing any Federal soldier that ventured out and stayed too long in the open.

The meeting had ended quickly because no place was safe in so far as the Biafrans were around. Secondly, they needed to get out of the place otherwise, they were all going to be dead people. It was a Sunday morning, the religious had just finished praying for God to deliver them from the hands of the Biafrans. Major Ted Hamman had just stepped outside, put his helmet on to avoid any of the Biafran snipers who were constantly lurking about blowing his head wide open. They were becoming good at shooting officers from a distance. As he bent forward, in an attempt not to make himself big enough for a target, he took a step forward. Something cut a sharp path across his left abdomen in a wet slap. There was a slice, which was followed by a stinging pain. Behind him, the bullet slammed into something. Metal shredded. Glass shattered,

Major Hamman screamed. All the Federal troops standing around dove to the ground as the belated sound of the rifle shot reverberated around the half-destroyed house they had used as a meeting place. Corporal Kyari, taking cover beside Major Hamman, shouted, "Oga, come oh! Oga come oh! Dem don kill Oga oh!" crawled to him, then grabbed him under the shoulders to pull him away to avoid a second shot.

Major Hamman felt agonizing pain as he realized the bullet had taken a chunk of his left side. His intestines, both large and small, including other internal organs that reminded him of a cut open cow were jumbled together in a gory soup as blood squirted everywhere. Corporal Kyari dragged him to the back of the shattered remnants of the building. Although it had been shelled heavily this morning, it was still intact enough to serve as the company's headquarters. Hamman's teeth were gritted in pain. His eyes were wild and mad. Colonel Etuk ran out to where Major Hamman lay gasping for breath. He took one look at his wound and knew right away that the man needed medical evacuation or he would bleed out in less than thirty minutes. The Brigade's desperation was vividly captured by Major Hamman's situation. The unit's doctor was right there on the spot but basically useless with no drugs and no equipment to do his job right. The doctor simply took a brown t-shirt to hold the intestines in.

PART FIVE

Colonel Etuk stood, chewing his lower lip as he watched his assistant slowly bleeding to death right in front of his eyes. He knew he could do nothing about it. Then, Major Hamman said, "Oga, Allah, Allah, if I see Adekunle I will finish him. Adekunle is the man that has caused this.

Colonel Etuk said, "Well, we cannot say, but all we should be thinking is to be able to leave this place if it is possible."

He tried to sit up; "Kai, that hurts," he said.

Then, gunfire erupted all around them like a battalion of angry wasps. Every one dove to the floor. The Biafrans were at it again.

As they all lay on the ground, Corporal Kyari asked Major Hamman, "Where are you hit?"

"I don't know. Everywhere," Hamman said through clenched teeth. The possibility of dying had never been something that he spent a lot of time worrying about. To him, the army was just a job to do. Major Hamman did not want to die. He didn't have some sick visualization of himself going out in a blaze of glory. Corporal Kyari checked the wound by lifting the brown t-shirt which was soaking wet with blood, then whistled when he saw the scary entry site of the high powered bullet of the sniper's rifle. The big gash was oozing blood on Major Hamman's side. He tried to sit back up but immediately grabbed the ribs on his left and winced. "I think they may have broken a rib or two," he said. It sounded like a blend between someone who was jovial and insane all at once.

Corporal Kyari said, "Someone will come get us out of here. They're probably on their way as we speak." Even, he was not convinced at what he said, but that was the best he could come up with, considering the circumstance.

Major Hamman let out an agonizing sigh. A sharp, stabbing pain radiated from the left side of his ribcage crawling up his shoulders and then down his thigh. He was pretty sure one of the ribs was broken and figured he must remain courageous to the rest of the team.

Corporal Kyari said, "Well, if they are on their way, they'll need to get here soon. And if they don't, we'll have to make our move."

Then, Major Hamman took a long, painful breath and gave a long sigh that sounded like the air going slowly out of a punctured tire, all the way, until there was nothing left. He died. This was the cue that the remnants of the 16th Brigade were waiting for. They piled into their vehicles, armoured cars and trucks prepared to fight their way out of the city even with the Biafrans snapping at their heels.

X   X   X

As the 16th Brigade of the Federal 3rd Division decided Owerri was no longer viable and they must leave town in a hurry, the Biafrans were saddened their source of supply was leaving, but they still gave chase...

Obi watched in horror. He could only shake his head at his impotence at the moment. A man was being tortured right before his eyes. The electric wire tying the man's hands tightly behind him had bitten deep into his wrists so that his swollen skin had become corrugated—a sign that he had been so tied for several days. Dressed only in his boxers, he looked to be 30, maybe 32 and had a neat haircut atop a handsome face. That was all. The mob was infuriated. Two stalwart men propped him up against a pine electric pole and started punching him in the stomach. He was too weak to even scream. He fell sideways like a sack of beans and landed in a heap. The two men stood him up again. The one gave him an uppercut which snapped his head up as something white and laced with blood, flew out of his mouth. Blood mixed with spittle poured from his mouth as his head lolled like that of a rag doll.

A little girl came forward brandishing a twig with a forked pointed tip and stabbed him on the side. The crowd looked on. Then, the stalwart men looped a rope around him to keep him in place at the base of the electric pole and stepped back. This served as a cue, and all attached him. An old man lifted a nine-inch cinder block and smashed it on his head. The block dissolved in shards of sand and powdered cement. A woman hit him in the groin which made him double up and mutter, "Mercy, please."

In the distance, a policeman took one look at what was going on, shook his head and walked the opposite way. A tall, skinny man pulled out a dagger and made a sharp slashing swipe across his stomach revealing a side to side gash that suddenly turned crimson and bulged, threatening to spill his innards. He said, "Mercy..." again, but no one was listening to him. He was nyamiri and his brothers had killed their spiritual leader. All of them are the same— aggressive, all grabbing, and wanting it all. He must die on behalf of his brothers. This had been Mr. Obi's brother. It was to be his turn next. He had been made to watch as his brother was tortured to death. At the time, he had been too weak to understand the enormity of what he was looking at.

Several weeks after his miraculous escape, he was back in Ibo land reliving the experience. His escape was in deed miraculous. Some soldiers had come up to them and taken them to a bush where there were to be used for target practice. They had been an order for them to be lined up at the edge of the bush nearby and shot. Immediately, the soldiers pulled back the cocking handles of the automatic weapons, they had started running towards the bush. They were all mowed down in a brutal slaughter. A bullet had hit him on the left shoulder blade in an impact that felt like a solid kick from a cow, knocking him down. He had passed out and did not know what happened after that. He had woken up when a sprinkling of sand fell on him. They had been an attempt to cover the mass grave with sand not up to three inches thick. He had crawled out in the middle of the night and spent a nightmarish two weeks of a back route way back to the Ibo enclave.

X   X   X

Mister Obi who had insisted he be called that way on an account he used to be a school teacher where everybody called him that. After his rehabilitation and the return of passable movement of his arm, he had joined BOFF, especially after he heard of their aim. BOFF was made up of pissed off people who had suffered any form of indignity from pogroms aimed at people of eastern Nigerian extraction. He had an axe to grind with the Federals.

With his education and level of maturity, he rose to become a BOFF leader. Today, he was planning for his sector with his men. Surrounded by dangerous men whose only reason for fighting as a retaliatory strike against a people who had wronged them in a painfully unfair manner.

Mister Obi said to the squad of men, "You job is to act as the tripwire, to alert us to any attack from the south. If you encounter hostile Federal forces, you are to first determine strength and disposition, then break contact and report." They stared at him. "And then, you will transform from tripwire to caltrop. Pester and delay the Federal troops as much as possible during their advance until reinforcements arrive."

The men were ready and eager; and Mister Obi said, "Our group would supplement the army's squadron. We're to strike out in a north-westerly bearing, cross the Biafran demarcation line, and cause as much havoc as possible over the next 72 hours, in the hopes of distracting the federal forces and diverting some of their manpower away from the Owerri siege corridor... "

Unknown to Mister Obi and his men, the Federal 16th Brigade in Owerri wanted out and were going to shoot their way out. Unfortunately for them, they had chosen Mister Obi's sector as their route of escape.

And so, as elements of the retreating federal 16th Brigade which had decided to shoot its way out of

Owerri came upon Mister Obi's position, trouble started. He had commandeered a 20mm Breda anti-aircraft gun. The auto-cannon fired explosive shells from a twelve-round clip, and Obi had used it to terrifying effect against a squad of Federal troops charging their position. Mister Obi had thought the charge was an attack, not knowing that that had been a Federal squad sent to create a diversion for their general attempt at trying to fight their way out of captivity. The Breda Model 35 was a 20mm gas-operated anti-aircraft gun that fired at the rate of 240 rounds per minute.

Most of the squad had been blown apart by the shells, the few survivors huddled prostrate in the steaming offal that had been their comrade moments before. Obi had laughed at the carnage created, and had then used the Breda to shred the side of their truck, ripping apart the heavy metal tail gates and blasting fist-sized holes in them.

After the attack, the BOFF had come back to strip the Federal convoy of anything useful, taking their weapons, ammunition, explosives, food, fuel, spare parts, and even vehicles. The convoy had one armoured car up front and a Land Rover and one 4-ton lorry carrying all kinds of left over usable stuff, and while the troop carriers and trucks had been badly damaged to ever drive again, the others were repairable. Using the good vehicles, the rest of the repairable ones were towed and everything was brought back to base, including those heavy weapons that still worked. The BOFF were not always well-armed, but the firepower acquired in the encounter would make a significant difference if they had to engage any more Federal armoured vehicles in the near future. Of course, there every likelihood they'd be at the forefront of most of the encounters, the "if" of engaging the Federal forces was more likely a "when".

X   X   X

Owerri was recaptured. And the war, continued. ..